The Master of Mazes

The Master of Mazes

BY CAROL GASKIN

Illustrations by T. Alexander Price

TROLL ASSOCIATES

Library of Congress Cataloging in Publication Data

Gaskin, Carol.
The master of mazes.

(The Forgotten forest)
Summary: As a dweller in the Forgotten Forest, the reader makes decisions determining the course of the story after his pet beast becomes trapped in the manor house of the Master of Mazes.
1. Children's stories, American. 2. Plot-your-own stories. [1. Fantasy. 2. Plot-your-own stories]
I. Price, T. Alexander, ill. II. Title. III. Series:
Gaskin, Carol. Forgotten forest.
PZ7.G213Mas 1985 [Fic] 84-24015
ISBN 0-8167-0322-1 (lib. bdg.)
ISBN 0-8167-0323-X (pbk.)

Printed in the United States of America.

10 9 8 7 6 5 4 3 2 1

Welcome to the Forgotten Forest

In this adventure, your best friend has wandered onto the estate of the mysterious Master of Mazes. Now your friend may be lost, or trapped, and you must try to rescue him. But there is magic and danger everywhere.

Start your quest on page 1, and keep reading till you come to a choice. After that, the story is up to you. Your decisions will take you from page to page.

Think carefully before you decide! Some choices will lead you to exciting, heroic, and happy endings. But other choices can quickly lead to disaster.

No matter how your adventure turns out, you can always go back to the beginning and follow a new path. Choose well, and the best of luck in your quest!

1

"What a perfect day for tristle-hunting," you think to yourself, pulling a woolen cap over your shaggy hair and hooking a basket on your arm. "Come on, Redfern, let's go!" you call. Your pet bounds happily after you.

An early frost has come and gone. The late-afternoon air is crisp and clear, and the earth smells of fallen leaves. Leaving behind your home among the forest dwellers, you set out along the neglected road that leads to Shiver Wood.

Redfern trots cheerfully at your side. Ruffling his yellow fur, you think back to the days before he came into your life. How long ago it seems! Always up before dawn, always cold. . . . A forest dweller's life was hard then, and a tristler's job was hardest of all.

Tristles—the rarest of delicacies, strange, purple fruits—grow underground near oak-tree roots, concealed from sight. They ripen only in the winter. So every winter—before Redfern came—you spent long days examining the roots of trees and poking through the frozen forest floor.

Each spring, the tristlers would make a long trek to the cave-dwelling gnomes who lived in the mountains at the edge of the Forgotten Forest. There they would trade their crops for tools and foodstuffs, jewels and gold.

And in summer, the tristlers would explore new forests, braving the dangers that all travelers in strange lands must face—pirates and brigands, dragons and sorcerers.

It takes a special kind of person to be a tristler—hearty and patient, adventurous and brave. Your family has always followed this ancient trade, and you are proud to bear the name "Lin the Tristler."

But the rigors of a tristler's life left little time for building cottages, planting gardens, schooling, and the like. Finally, one grim winter almost a year ago, there were no tristles to be found.

There was but one place left to look: Shiver Wood. The forest dwellers had always avoided this place for fear of enchantment. But you could see its great oaks rising in the distance, and one cold morning, off you went.

Shiver Wood was not unlike the forests of your homeland. Noticing a series of holes in the ground, as though another tristler was about, you followed the telltale signs and suddenly came upon a most peculiar beast. He was snuffling along the ground, trailing leaves from his fuzzy yellow fur, his nose sweeping the earth before him like a wagging tail. His snout was as large as an anteater's, and his ears were pointed like a donkey's. Nose twitching, he stopped to dig with his oversize paws. Then, with twinkling eyes, he presented you with a perfect tristle.

"Who are you?" you asked in amazement. But the beast could not speak. Instead he plucked at your sleeve.

"Shirt?" you guessed. He shook his head.

"Red?" Yes, that was it. Your shirt was red. Next he pulled a leafy plant from the ground.

"Fern?" He nodded. "Red Fern?" Yes. And so you had met Redfern.

The beast proved to be as comfortable on two legs as on four. Walking with one of his furry arms thrown casually across your shoulder, he pointed to the sights of interest in Shiver Wood—a peetro bird, a woodland elf. Then, his ears pricking up and his nose quivering, he dropped to all fours and began to dig. In no time, he had located two dozen tristles, each of which he deposited in your basket with a satisfied nod.

Later that day you had wandered deep into Shiver Wood when all at once the sky darkened as though a blanket of thunderclouds had been drawn across the trees. Woodbats! Catching your scent, the screeching bats began to dive in your direction. Before you knew what was happening, Redfern had pushed you under a nearby bush and rubbed a tristle into your hair. Throwing another tristle at a swooping bat, he too ducked under the bush and gestured for you to be still.

"False alarm, raiders!" squeaked the attacking bat. "It's only Redfern." Fooled by the scent of the tristles, the bat swerved away, leading the swarm to patrol elsewhere.

"That was close," you said with a shiver. "I can see where this wood gets its name. Thank you, Redfern. I guess I'd better go back home. Will you show me the way out of this wood?"

Redfern guided you safely to the edge of Shiver Wood, pausing occasionally to dig a tristle or two. Then, when your basket was full, he accompanied you home. He has stayed with you ever since. And your life has never been the same.

There is no other creature like Redfern. He may be as single-minded as an anteater and as stubborn as a donkey, but he has proved to be affectionate and loyal above all. With his help, you can find enough tristles to support your whole family in a fraction of the time it used to take. A tristle market has opened in a nearby town, and now you have spare time to read and to play.

Though Redfern has a nose for tristles, he can't seem to smell much else. The other forest dwellers believe he must have been a "mistake" on the part of a young wizard's apprentice learning to make beasts. But you don't care what he is. He is now your best friend.

Today is a day for tristling if there ever was one. With Redfern to guide you, you are eager to explore a secluded clearing you remember from your day in Shiver Wood. Your fright with the bats is long past, and your curiosity has been building for months.

A walk of several hours brings the two of you to the edge of the clearing. It is much larger than you remembered. Following Redfern's skillful nose, you discover a grassy track, rutted as though from cart-wheels.

Redfern trots ahead of you, his nose to the ground, and you hurry after him. The track winds and bumps, passing through the clearing and into an open field.

In the distance you catch sight of a wooden cart. It is trundling toward a curious gate in a huge, moss-covered wall.

The gate swings open, just as you recognize the cart's cargo. It is laden with fresh tristles. Redfern takes off after it!

"Redfern, *wait*!" you call. "Come back!" But your cries are to no avail. Redfern, hot on the scent of the precious tristles, follows the cart beyond the wall, and the gate slams closed.

Running to the gate, you shout, "Redfern, come back!" There is no answer. You try the gate, but it is locked.

A dull bronze plaque peeks through the moss on the wall. Rubbing it clean with your sleeve, you read MASTER OF MAZES.

You settle down to wait for the cart to come out again. If Redfern has not returned by then, you will go in after him.

You have little chance to wonder what lies beyond the gate. For you hear the hollow rumbling of an empty cart and flatten yourself against the wall, ready to spring.

The gate swings open and the cart thunders through, drawn by a dappled horse. The driver, a mountain gnome, does not notice you. And Redfern is nowhere in sight.

With one nimble hop, you are within the mysterious walls. The gate slams closed behind you.

Turn to page 8.

from page 6

A great manor house rises before you. In all of your travels, you have never seen such a large and confusing building. Wings shoot off from every side. There are turrets and balconies, gables and porches. At the back there appears to be a formal garden, and the forested grounds stretch as far as you can see, ringed by the towering wall.

There is no one about.

Should you head for the grounds at the back of the house and search for your friend in the forest? Or should you announce yourself at the manor house and try to find the mysterious Master of Mazes? Perhaps he has already made a friend of Redfern. Or a prisoner.

If you head for the grounds, turn to page 13.

If you enter the manor house, turn to page 16.

from page 26

You study the puzzle. The letters in the words GANDER and DANGER, rearRANGED, spell GARDEN.

This clue must be telling you to search the garden!

Turn to page 31.

from page 46

Looking closely at your clue, you notice that some of the letters are underlined. They spell LOOSE HAYSEED.

Now you can see that the blue ribbon had concealed a seam in the neck of the porcelain goose. With a single twist, the head pulls off, and you find that the statuette is indeed full of loose hayseed.

You decide to search the rest of the house for Redfern. But the door you came through has disappeared.

I *know* there was a door in this wall, you think, feeling along the plaster surface for a hidden latch. Suddenly a door appears where before there was none. But you still haven't found any latch. And just as suddenly, the door vanishes completely as another door appears farther along the wall.

This time you see your chance and run through the door before it can start to disappear.

You are in a maze of appearing and disappearing doors.

Leaving your route to chance, you pass through one door after another. But you cleverly dribble a handful of hayseed to mark your trail, in case you must find your way back.

Turn to page 18.

from page 84

This must be another word game, you think. You study the lettering of the clue. If the word SHALT were not in the word LABYRINTHS, would you find a name? Eliminating letters one by one, you subtract an S, an H, an A, an L, and a T.

"BYRIN," you say out loud.

"You are clever indeed, Lin the Tristler," says a voice behind the labyrinth door. "Byrin it is."

A princely-looking man with a curly brown beard steps through the door. He is dressed in a brocade jacket patterned after the design in the floor.

"I hope you have enjoyed your stay in my house," he says. "Now you may name your prize."

"I claim only my companion, Redfern," you answer modestly, "and safe conduct back to your gates."

"Granted," says Byrin. He steps aside, and Redfern runs joyfully from the labyrinth. "I have greatly enjoyed your company," says Byrin. "I hope you will visit me often. You have the makings of a Master of Mazes yourself, you know."

"Thank you," you answer. "Let's go home, Redfern," you say to your friend. He looks embarrassed to have caused you such trouble. "Never mind, Redfern," you say. "It's been worth it."

And, dreaming of the mazes *you* may build someday, you set off for home.

THE END

from page 71

You have lost patience with the Master of Mazes and his riddles. You dash the crystal to the floor. *Smash!* The crystal shatters, and bits of glass and snow fly everywhere. But the tiny figure that looks like you begins to stretch and grow!

Soon you are staring in amazement at your exact double. But this other Lin, who does not seem to see you, turns to walk away.

"Wait!" you say, waving your arms. "You're *me.*" There is no response.

Your silent twin circles the study, peering at books and paintings and examining the walls. You trail along, curious to see what the other Lin is looking for.

Suddenly you pause before a large oil painting. It is a portrait of Redfern! Your twin keeps walking, but you stop to examine the painting. Redfern is standing upright in a noble pose. As you touch the frame, searching for an artist's signature, the painting swings aside, uncovering a door.

On the opposite side of the room, your double presses a panel in the wall. The panel slides open, revealing a secret passage.

If you want to follow your double through the secret passage, turn to page 37.

If you want to open the door behind the painting, turn to page 98.

from page 8

There is no sign of the owner of the manor. You decide that Redfern has probably stayed outdoors to go tristling.

"Redfern!" you call, wandering around to the back of the house. Where could he have gone?

You are walking along a thick wall of hedges about shoulder high. Beyond the hedge, in a formal garden, flower beds have been planted. They make colorful pictures with their blooms, despite the season.

Searching for an entrance to the garden, you come upon an opening cut in the hedge wall. A white-pebbled path leads away from the wall, to a forested area some distance from the manor.

If you want to enter the garden, turn to page 31.

If you want to search in the forest, turn to page 24.

from page 88/from page 107

The smell of tristles is coming from behind a little wooden door. You pull it open to find a storeroom filled with tristles. But there is no sign of Redfern.

You stuff a few of the tristles into your pockets among the red beans. Perhaps Redfern will smell them and find you.

At the back of the storeroom is another door. It leads to a maze of underground tunnels.

On a table just inside the entrance, you find a dripping candle and a glowing lantern. A sign at the end of the table says TAKE ONE.

If you take the candle, turn to page 40.

If you take the lantern, turn to page 25.

If you take them both, turn to page 44.

from page 8

You decide to search the manor house first. A brass knocker hangs on a freshly painted white door. You lift the knocker to rap several times, and the door swings open in answer to your echoing knock.

There is not a soul in sight as you enter a sun-filled hall, squinting against the bright light.

The manor door clicks shut behind you, and you turn to see a message pinned to the inside of the door:

Those with manners
Knock doors.
Those with manors
Lock doors.

You have been locked in!

Sunlight streams through oval windows set high above the ground floor. Everything is white, and the walls seem to be made of paper.

As you watch, the walls begin to change position, sliding across the floor, like screens. Beyond them you can see more shifting walls. They open and close, and make a maze of momentary rooms and passages.

For an instant you can see all the way to the back of the house and out to the garden. You glimpse a yellow shape.

"Redfern!" you shout.

But the passageway has disappeared, and a new arrangement of halls and rooms has appeared in its place.

Poking a finger through the nearest partition, you find that it is indeed made of paper.

If you want to follow the maze as the screens slide open and closed, turn to page 33.

If you want to burst through the paper walls to the back of the house, turn to page 26.

from page 10

Open, slam! Open, slam! Finally the maze of doors spews you out into a vast, mirrored ballroom.

No longer are there lines of doors, only repeating reflections of yourself. You look small and pale beneath huge chandeliers that hang from a ceiling painted with stars.

At one end of the ballroom a marble staircase sweeps grandly to the heights of the house. And in a draped alcove to your left, a table is elegantly laid with tea and cakes. It seems your host has regained his manners!

A breeze stirs the drapery, and a slip of paper rustles on the tea tray. You read:

You rest for tea and try to decipher the picture code.

If you think the message is to take the staircase, turn to page 92.

If you think the clue is about seeing stars, turn to page 42.

from page 39/from page 83

The wind has stirred up the forest floor, burying the tristle holes under fallen leaves. Acorns seem to be everywhere. But here and there a gleaming white marker shows the way. You are glad you used the pebbles!

Following the bright white dots through the maze of tree roots, you find the edge of the forest. Soon you are back at the opening in the hedge wall.

This time you decide to search the garden.

Turn to page 31.

from page 24

Ta-roo! You hear the sound of the hunting horn again and set off toward it. Just beyond a stand of pines you come upon a knight. He holds a golden hunting horn to his lips. *Ta-taroo!*

"Hello!" you cry, covering your ears. "That's loud!"

"I beg your pardon," says the knight, setting down his horn. "I am hoping a friend of mine will hear my signal. I am searching for my tristling beast, you see, lost these many months."

Your heart flutters. Could he mean Redfern?

"Are you the Master of Mazes?" you ask the knight.

"Dear me, no!" he replies. "I am Sir Alf of Redfern. The Master of Mazes is an evil rogue, I hear tell. And you'd best be careful, for I fear we are trespassing on his land. But you look able. Would you like to join my search?"

Sir Alf seems friendly enough. But what is his claim to Redfern?

If you want to travel with Sir Alf, turn to page 110.

If you want to travel by yourself and try to find Redfern first, turn to page 51.

from page 84

You enter the labyrinth. It is a honeycomb of six-sided rooms that all look the same. But some have only one arched door; others have two or three, or even more.

You wander for hours until you come to a sign that says CLUE 2:

When in LABYRINTHS
Take the first two LANES
And the last three PATHS.

If you can guess the Master of Mazes' name from this clue, turn to page 36.

If you want to look for the first two lanes and the last three paths, turn to page 78.

from page 48

You start to retrace your steps, turning first to the right, then left, then right again.

But wait a minute—this couldn't be the way you came. Where is the entrance to the maze? And now there are three choices rather than two. This passageway has two left turns, and another to the right.

You try one of the passageways, but come to a dead end. The walls around you all look the same.

There is no doubt about it. You are lost in a green-marble maze.

THE END

from page 13

Guessing that Redfern has gone to the forest, you set out on the white-pebbled path. Along the way you decide to fill your pockets with pebbles. They may come in handy for marking your trail in a manor of mazes.

The path peters out, and the trees get larger and larger. Some of the trees are mighty oaks, and there are acorns everywhere. Other trees spring from twisted roots that arch high above the ground like giant birdcages. The wood grows thick and eerie.

Soon you are in a dense maze of tree roots. It is as though the airless underground world has pushed its way to the earth's surface.

Here and there you spot the telltale marks of a tristler: Holes have been dug recently among the tree roots.

Suddenly the blast of a hunting horn shatters the quiet. Could the Master of Mazes be hunting nearby?

If you want to head toward the sound of the hunting horn, turn to page 20.

If you want to follow the tristle holes, turn to page 38.

from page 14

Choosing the lantern, you wander through the maze of tunnels. For safety's sake, you decide to leave a trail of beans in your path so you can find your way out again.

When you reach a dead end, you mark the tunnel with a small pile of beans, then take another route.

Someone patters up behind you. You turn and meet a furry form. Redfern! And is he glad to see you!

After embracing your friend, you retrace your steps to the storeroom.

You didn't need the trail of beans after all, because Redfern's nose leads you directly to the tristles.

Entering the storeroom, you find yourselves face to face with the Master of Mazes. The princely man is calmly munching a tristle, waiting for you to appear.

"Well done, Lin and Redfern," he says happily. "You have mastered my mazes, solved my puzzles, followed my clues, and won my little game.

"Here is your reward—your freedom, and a year's supply of tristles!"

THE END

from page 17

You decide to take the direct route to the back of the house. After all, paper walls are easy to fix.

You break through one flimsy screen after another, hoping you are moving in a straight line. It is not easy to tell, when the walls shift about so much.

But with a final burst of tearing paper, you reach the back of the house. You are in a large, airy room lined with windows. French doors lead to a terrace, and beyond that you can see well-kept gardens, hen houses, and a stable. There is no trace of Redfern.

As you gaze out the windows, another message, neatly printed on white paper, flutters to your feet:

Take a GANDER
RearRANGED
Signs of DANGER
Will be changed!

What kind of game is this maze master playing? you wonder. This must be a clue. Let's see. A gander is a male goose—but how can you rearrange a goose?

If you think you should look for a goose in the hen houses, turn to page 46.

If you think the answer is in the garden, turn to page 9.

from page 106

Deciding you'd better get out before you freeze, you grab the toboggan and brush the snow from its padded surface. Then you sit at the back of the flat-bottomed sled with your legs straight out before you. At the front the sled curves up and inward, and there are handrails to steer with on either side.

You shift your weight, and the sled lurches onto the icy track. The hill slopes gently at first, but soon you pick up speed. The narrow sled zips down the hill, crunching loudly on the ice. Frozen pellets of ice break loose and fly past your face as you hurtle downward at top speed.

An icy wall looms before you! You shift your weight and the toboggan turns, narrowly missing the wall. Another turn! You shift again!

You are moving so fast that everything is a white blur. The toboggan track is a maze of sudden curves and hidden turns. You are almost flat on your back in the sled, and you steer more by instinct than by sight.

Thinking you must be almost to the bottom of the hill, you relax just for an instant. But look out—a dead end!

Twisting sharply, you avoid a crash. But your sled overturns on top of you, and you tumble over and over. At last you slide roughly to a stop.

Opening your eyes, you roll the toboggan away and pull yourself to your feet. Something white crunches under your feet. But it is not cold and it is not snow.

You are standing on the white-pebbled path that leads to the gardens! At your back, where moments ago you hurtled down a steep hill, looms the manor house of the Master of the Mazes. But is that a bit of snow melting on an attic windowsill?

You enter the gardens and follow the white-pebbled path past benches and fountains. The path winds toward a towering maze of manicured hedges, some of them clipped in animal shapes—a topiary zoo.

You stop at a bench to rest. You are not sure you are ready to tackle yet another maze.

Suddenly a flash of yellow catches your eye. Redfern! But why is he rushing into the hedge maze? You call after him, but he doesn't seem to hear you.

If you race after Redfern, turn to page 79.

If you first fill your pockets with pebbles, turn to page 122.

from page 34

You decide to follow the clockwork dancer. She whirs through the door as you open it and leads you to a mirrored ballroom. Sparkling chandeliers hang from a ceiling painted with stars. The ballerina circles around you and seems to invite you to join her. But you are in no mood to dance with a toy.

"I'm tired of this silly game," you say aloud to the empty ballroom. "Where is Redfern?"

The ballerina spins slowly, her gears winding down. At the end of the ballroom she rests, quite still, at the foot of a grand marble staircase.

In a draped alcove to your left, a small table is set with tea and cakes. A breeze stirs the drapery, and something white rustles on the tea tray. A message!

Picking up the piece of paper, you read:

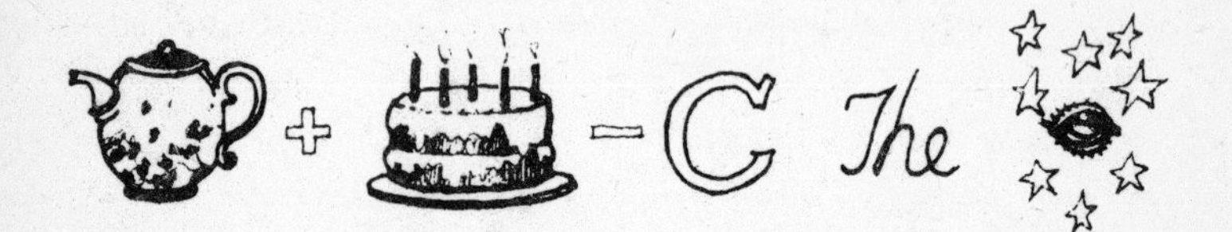

If you think the message has to do with the staircase, turn to page 92.

If you think the clue has to do with seeing stars, turn to page 42.

from page 9/from page 13/from page 19

The gardens are magnificent. Flowers bloom in autumn, and all have been planted to make fantastical designs on the sprawling lawns. Strange sundials nestle in secret groves, and statues on pedestals decorate avenues of weeping willows.

The manor house rises behind you. Two urns mark the beginning of a broad path that leads to a fountain. And at the center of the fountain is a statue of—Redfern!

If there is only one such beast in the world, you think, how did this get here? The Master of the Mazes must *know* Redfern.

You study the statue of your friend. A stream of water trickles from his marble mouth, and one paw points to a gazebo—a small, open structure—a short distance away.

If you want to take a drink from the fountain, turn to page 41.

If you head for the gazebo, turn to page 80.

from page 60/from page 115

You steal quietly into the manor house, wandering from room to room.

Inside, the house is even more confusing than it appeared from the outside. Staircases lead to solid walls; doors open onto chutes and tunnels; furniture trots about on animal feet.

You enter a paneled chamber on an upper floor. Walking to a window, you can see that you are at the back of the house, for the gardens and hedge maze are below you. You look for Sir Alf, hoping he is lost, so you can find Redfern first.

But two figures are wandering in the hedge maze, *both* of them lost. One is Redfern! And close behind him is Sir Alf! They are sure to find each other soon. You turn to race out of the room.

Pounding on the paneled walls, you shout for help as the cackling of the Master of Mazes echoes around you. For now the paneling is solid, and the chamber no longer has any doors.

You will have to watch the reunion of Sir Alf and Redfern from your window.

THE END

from page 17

The Master of Mazes, whoever he may be, must enjoy confusing his visitors. Deciding to follow your host's lead for the time being, you enter the maze of sliding white walls.

Zigzagging through the spaces created as the paper panels shift right or left, you soon reach a set of double doors. They are made of wood, and are quite solid.

Beyond the doors you find yourself in a small chamber that is filled with musical instruments. There is a harpsichord with a scene of a masquerade painted on its open lid. A silver flute rests on a music stand, and a cello leans against one wall. But most remarkable is a life-size clockwork ballerina, frozen in mid-step, a large silver key in her back.

On the floor, an intricate pattern of contrasting woods forms a pathway of arrows that point through an archway and into a hall on your right.

You are about to follow the arrow designs when you hear a few tinkling notes of music. And is it your imagination, or did the ballerina blink? You look again, and she cocks her head to one side like a curious bird.

Curious yourself, you turn the key in her back to wind her up. A music-box waltz begins to play. Then, taking several jerky steps, she executes a wobbly pirouette on one pointed toe. With much whirring and clicking of her clockwork gears, she dances across the floor, then stops, pointing to a door on your left.

If you follow the mechanical ballerina, turn to page 30.

If you follow the pattern in the floor, turn to page 84.

from page 22

Perhaps this is another word game, you think, noticing a similarity in the capitalized words. What if I take the first two *letters* in LANES and the last three in PATHS?

"LATHS," you say aloud. Nothing happens. Perhaps if I *take* the letters *away* from the word LABYRINTHS? You subtract the letters one by one: L, A, T, H, S.

"BYRIN," you say aloud.

"Byrin is indeed my name," says the Master of Mazes from the shadow of an archway. "Solve it in two, your friend will join you."

Redfern scampers into the room, almost knocking you over with delight. By the time you recover from your joyful reunion, the shadowy figure is gone.

You have found your friend. But you still have to find your way out of the maze.

THE END

from page 12

Deciding to trail your mysterious double, you quickly duck into the passage just before the panel slides shut behind you. Although the passage is dark, you can make out the form of your twin rounding a corner at the end of the passage.

Hurrying to follow, you closely shadow the phantom Lin through several dim corridors.

Suddenly the passageway ahead of your double is flooded with light, casting a long shadow toward you. You feel as though you are lengthening and floating along the floor. Your head feels foggy and weightless.

As your double nears the light, you can feel yourself flatten and shrink! How have you got so close to your strange twin's feet?

As the light dims again, you understand what has happened: You have turned into your own shadow, a shadow of yourself.

You wonder what will become of you when the light goes out.

THE END

from page 24

Preferring to avoid whoever is hunting, you concentrate on finding Redfern. But the tristle holes lead deeper and deeper into the maze of tree roots. Soon you may be lost.

You decide to mark your path through the forest. Your pockets are filled with white pebbles, but what if you need them farther along? Acorns are certainly plentiful. But they won't show up as well as pebbles. Acorns or pebbles? You must choose.

Setting out through the maze of tree roots, you drop the marker of your choice every three or four paces. Sometimes you have to walk a long way between tristle holes. There is no sign of Redfern.

Finally, you run out of markers. And you don't think you'd better go on without them. Nearby is a mound of earth, piled in a clearing. It seems to be *rippling*—or are your eyes playing tricks?

Drawing closer, you find the mound to be an enormous anthill. Millions of ants are streaming up and down its sides, in and out of tunnels. Some carry bits of leaf and other treasures. All seem extremely busy.

A flash of light catches your eye, and you bend to pick up a small glass bottle. The label reads:

TRANSFORMATION SPELL

Be an ant.

15 min.

The bottle is tightly corked, and you can see that it is half full of greenish liquid—or half empty. Could Redfern have swallowed some of this?

You are not sure you want to be an ant. Perhaps it's time to turn back to the manor. The wind is blowing and you feel chilled. But the spell would last only fifteen minutes . . . .

If you want to return to the manor, and you marked your path with acorns, turn to page 117.

If you want to turn back, and you chose white pebbles, turn to page 19.

If you want to stay and try the transformation spell, turn to page 54.

from page 14

Choosing the candle, you wander into the maze of tunnels. The wax drips along your path, leaving white marks as you zigzag and turn.

Suddenly you hear a scuffling noise ahead of you. Someone is running in your direction. It is Redfern!

Hugging you happily, he pulls a tristle from your pocket. Then he nearly drags you back to the storeroom, guided by the trail of wax. Or is it the scent of tristles he is following?

For as you get closer to the storeroom, Redfern starts to act a little funny. He bumps into a wall. He giggles. He hiccups.

Emerging into the storeroom, you catch sight of the mountain gnome you saw at the gate. He is just disappearing with an empty cart.

You have never seen so many tristles all in one place! The gnome must have unloaded another cartful while you were in the tunnel maze.

And Redfern is overwhelmed by the scent. He rolls dizzily on the floor. You have never seen him like this before. And you still have to find a way out of here!

If you want to trail the mountain gnome, turn to page 65.

If you want to stay with Redfern, turn to page 97.

from page 31

You kneel at the fountain to take a drink. The manor house behind you is reflected in the pool of water.

Cupping your hands, you splash some water on your face. Your movements send a wave of ripples through the reflection of the manor.

But what is that wavy yellow shape you see in one of the upper windows? Could it be Redfern? Or was it just a trick of the sunlight?

You whirl around to look at the house, but the sun strikes your eyes. The yellow shape has vanished.

If you want to continue your search in the manor house, turn to page 72.

If you head for the gazebo, turn to page 80.

from page 18/from page 30

Maybe the clue has to do with seeing stars and maybe it doesn't, but your attention is drawn to the fluttering drapery at the window. Could it be night already? Are the stars out?

You draw aside the curtain. It is still broad daylight. You are looking down on a formal garden planted at the foot of several flagstone terraces. In the garden is a hedge maze, and from your vantage point, two stories above, you can see the pattern of its paths.

Someone is wandering in the maze. It is Redfern! But there is another figure in the maze as well. He has the body of a man and the head of a bull—a minotaur! The monster is carrying a deadly mace and is separated from Redfern by only a single hedge.

"Run, Redfern!" you shout. "No, not that way—it's a dead end!" But Redfern cannot hear you. You watch, helpless, as your friend is stalked by the monster. Could he be the Master of Mazes? You must get to the garden to save your friend!

You try the windows, but they are all sealed. And it is a sheer drop to the flagstone terraces below.

If you want to bang on the glass to try to distract the minotaur, turn to page 58.

If you want to search for a way to the garden, turn to page 112.

from page 14

Why should I take just *one*? you think. It's dark in the tunnel.

Entering the eerie maze, you hold the candle in one hand and the lantern in the other. They make a lot of light, and you can see quite well.

Suddenly you hear a loud screeching. Where have I heard that noise before? you wonder. Then you remember. *Woodbats!*

A thousand woodbats swoop through the tunnel, disturbed by the bright light. Trying to cover your ears against their shrieks, you drop the candle, and it goes out with a puff.

The beating of bat wings makes a gush of air that rattles the glass of the lantern. The light sputters out.

You are swamped in darkness, lost in a maze with a swarm of deadly woodbats.

THE END

from page 72/from page 92

The minutes pass slowly as you wait for the grandfather clock to strike the hour. Then you will know what the clock has to say.

Tick, tock. Tick, tock. The pendulum swings to and fro. Tick, tock.

The hour hand jumps into place, and the clock begins to strike.

But wait. *That's* what a clock says before "a tock." "A tick"! *Attic.*

Bong! bong! bong! You are about to head for the attic when the striking clock falls silent and a little door pops open. A mechanical animal hands you a note.

TIME'S UP, says the note. You see with dismay that the clockwork animal looks just like Redfern.

THE END

from page 26

You are about to head for the hen houses when your eyes fall on a porcelain statuette of a goose, sitting at the center of a small table. It is decorated with a pattern of pretty wildflowers and sports a blue ribbon tied in a bow around its neck.

Noticing letters on the bow, you untie it and read: WILD-GOOSE CHASE—YOUR GOOSE IS COOKED.

Another clue! But are you on a wild-goose chase? Should you look for a cooked goose?

If you decide to search for the kitchen, turn to page 88.

If you think the statuette holds another clue, turn to page 10.

from page 72/from page 92

What *does* a clock say before "a tock"? you wonder. Why, it says "a tick." *Attic!*

Hurrying up the wooden stairs to the attic, you enter a lofty workroom. The room is furnished with slanted drawing tables on which are pinned half-finished plans and charts. You see rulers and protractors, books of riddles and mathematical theories, miniature models of towers and bridges. One model is a maze of trap doors and tunnels. Another is a building constructed of string.

You are startled by a footstep behind you and turn to meet your host. Elegantly dressed in a brocade dressing gown, he is unmistakably the master of the manor.

"So, my uninvited guest, we meet at last," he says, smiling politely. "I am Byrin, the Maze-ician."

"I am honored to make your acquaintance, sir," you reply, nervously introducing yourself. "I am searching for my friend, Redfern."

"Ah, yes, your friend . . . ." Byrin nods absently. "But perhaps you are interested in architecture? Now that you have entered my house, you can be of some assistance to me." He ushers you to a concealed doorway that springs open at his touch. "I would like you to test my new labyrinth for me. I believe it to be a most ingenious design."

"Prodding you through the doorway, he thrusts a folded wad of paper into your hand.

"Here is a map to help you along. Good-bye for now."

The door clicks shut and you are left in a maze of green-marble passageways. Unfolding the map, you turn it this way and that, but are unable to find a spot that looks like where you are standing. The passageway you are in is straight, with turns leading off in right angles, while the lines on the map are all curves.

You decide to explore a bit. At the end of the passage you must turn either right or left. You choose the passageway to the right and continue, next turning left, then right again. Still the map is useless. You will have to find another way to keep track of your wanderings.

You decide to start again at the beginning of the maze. But which is the correct way to get back there?

If you take a left turn, then a right, then another left, turn to page 52.

If you turn right, then left, then right, turn to page 23.

from page 59

You duck behind a wardrobe and wait to see what the monster will do.

The minotaur strides into the room, munching a tristle. Has he harmed Redfern? He shuts the door behind him. But he doesn't seem to be looking for you.

"Enough of this game," he says to himself. "Let's play another." He walks to a cabinet and hangs up his mace. Then, to your wonder, he pulls the bull's head from his shoulders and packs it away in a trunk.

The Master of Mazes is a princely man—but a man, not a minotaur.

"Time for a mirror trick!" he says, giggling. "This will confuse them!"

Turning to an ornate mirror, he utters a spell.

"Magic mirror from the east,
Disguise me as a tristling beast."

Before your eyes, the Master of Mazes is transformed into—Redfern!

"Now for the hedge maze," he says, heading for the door.

If you follow him into the hedge maze, turn to page 62.

If you want to use the mirror yourself, turn to page 101.

from page 20

Finders, keepers, you think to yourself, deciding to look for Redfern on your own. You hope that you can find him before Sir Alf does.

But it is the Master of Mazes you are worried about the most. Didn't Sir Alf call him an evil rogue? What if Redfern is in danger?

Taking his leave to continue his own quest, Sir Alf of Redfern strides through the forest. He is heading for the Master of Mazes' garden.

But you hesitate, for near your feet you spot a fresh tristle hole. Another hole leads you deeper into the forest.

If you want to follow the tristle holes into the forest, turn to page 66.

If you want to trail Sir Alf to the garden, turn to page 60.

from page 48

Retracing your steps, you turn left, then right, then left. You made the correct choice! Ahead of you is the doorway to the attic loft, the entrance to the maze. You are not surprised to find it locked.

There must be a way to master this maze, you think. Perhaps I can mark the walls to keep track of where I have been. But the green-marble walls and floor prove too hard to scratch, and scuff marks from your shoes don't show.

You study your useless map once more. I could tear up the map to leave a trail, you think. But what if I need it later?

If you decide to tear up the map, turn to page 71.

If you think you should save the map, turn to page 111.

from page 110

You and Sir Alf scatter your pebbles through the thicket, trying to mark your trail. But the pebbles fall through the brambles and are buried among sticks and leaves.

Soon you are lost in an endless thicket. It is like being woven into a giant bird's nest.

"You'd better start slashing," you tell Sir Alf.

But it seems he already has. For behind you is a path of broken twigs. You try to follow Sir Alf's sword marks, but the thicket instantly grows back, engulfing you in a cocoon of sticks.

You hope that Sir Alf will pass your way again before he escapes.

THE END

from page 39

Here goes, you think, holding your nose and gulping the green liquid.

You would like to blink in surprise. But you have no eyelids.

"Why, I'm an ant!" you say.

"That's right. So move it, buddy," says a squeaky voice behind you. Startled, you join a line of ants pouring through an opening in the anthill.

Inside the ant tunnels, all is scurry and confusion. Never have you seen such a crowd, even on opening day at the marketplace. You'll never find Redfern in here!

Streams of ants are pushing this way and that. You will have to join the flow, or risk being trampled.

One line of ants is climbing upward. Each ant is carrying a deep-red stone that looks like a ruby chip.

Another ant line is marching empty-handed into a downward tunnel.

If you want to follow the stone-carrying ants, turn to page 57.

If you want to join the ants going downward, turn to page 107.

from page 106

You are not sure an icy toboggan ride would help you at all. You decide to stay where you are and wait for the blizzard to end.

You carve yourself an alcove in the snow bank that once was a couch, and crouch in your windbreak. Snow piles around your feet.

The blizzard shows no signs of letting up. The toboggan is buried, and you are no longer sure you remember where it is. The snow is mounting, and you feel cold and sleepy. For you, this may be . . .

THE END

from page 54

You join the line of ants trudging upward through sandy tunnels, bearing their precious burdens. Where could they be going with hundreds of rubies? you wonder.

"We're almost to the Queen's chamber," squeaks a voice up ahead. "Look your best!" Several ants pause to straighten their antennae. Others adjust their rubies to display the best side.

Entering a spacious chamber, you line up to pay your respects to the Queen. She is reclining on a throne, surrounded by ruby chips.

"My gracious subjects," says the royal ant, "please arrange the treasures to encircle my chamber. For I await a visit from the Master of Mazes."

The ants scurry to do her bidding.

"Why, he is here!" exclaims the Queen ant. "Come, come, dear sir. I know it is you, for you carry no ruby. Sit by me. I command it. You are very wicked to wait so long between visits."

There is no doubt about it. The Queen is talking to *you*. Two large guards stand ready to escort you to her throne. The Queen looks impatient.

If you want to go along with her mistake, turn to page 103.

If you want to explain your quest and ask about Redfern, turn to page 83.

from page 42

The minotaur could capture Redfern at any moment. By the time you find a way to the garden, you could be too late. You decide you'd better try to distract the monster from where you are. Maybe you can draw him away from the maze.

Banging on the windowpanes, you press your nose and mouth against the glass and make horrible faces. Both Redfern and the minotaur stop in their tracks and look skyward. You pound harder. They see you!

Angrily shaking his mace, the minotaur roars up at your window. He reverses his steps and begins to stride through the alleyways of the hedge maze. Now he is after *you*.

Redfern is lost in the maze and looks confused. But the minotaur clearly knows his way out. You study his route from your window two stories up, trying to memorize the pattern of twists and turns.

The minotaur emerges from the maze and heads for the left side of the flagstone terrace. You flee to your right, running out of the ballroom directly into a slippery corridor that slants downward like a slide. *Whooah!* You end up on the ground floor again.

There are doors everywhere. Opening one, you catch yourself teetering at the edge of an empty shaft. Another door leads to a snake pit. Finally you find a room that looks safe to hide in.

It is a musty storeroom, a combination costume shop and armory. Horned helmets and iron weapons are encased along the walls, and wardrobes and trunks overflow with garments of every description.

There are heavy footsteps in the corridor, and the jangling of an iron mace. The minotaur is coming your way!

If you want to arm yourself and stand battle, turn to page 102.

If you want to hide behind a wardrobe, turn to page 50.

from page 51

You trail Sir Alf from a safe distance and enter the garden just as he disappears into a towering maze of hedges.

To your right, the manor house beckons. There is no one else in sight.

If you want to search in the manor house, turn to page 32.

If you follow Sir Alf into the hedge maze, turn to page 68.

from page 74

Tossing the fruit to the hungry bear, you decide not to wait to see if he is satisfied.

You flee back down the muddy path and soon reach the point at which it branches. It looks as if you haven't been followed. But you had better not wait here to find out. You choose the path with the white pebbles.

Turn to page 82.

from page 50

Hurrying after the Master of Mazes—or Redfern—you follow him into the hedge maze. But he moves so quickly through the complicated maze that you lose him, and are soon lost yourself.

You try to remember the pattern of the maze you saw from the ballroom window. But the alleyways of greenery all look the same.

The alley you are in comes to a T. You look to your right—and here comes Redfern! Chased by another Redfern!

The first Redfern catches sight of you and clasps you in a friendly hug. And the second Redfern grabs the first!

Which one is the real Redfern?

If you pick the first Redfern, turn to page 109.

If you pick the second Redfern, turn to page 114.

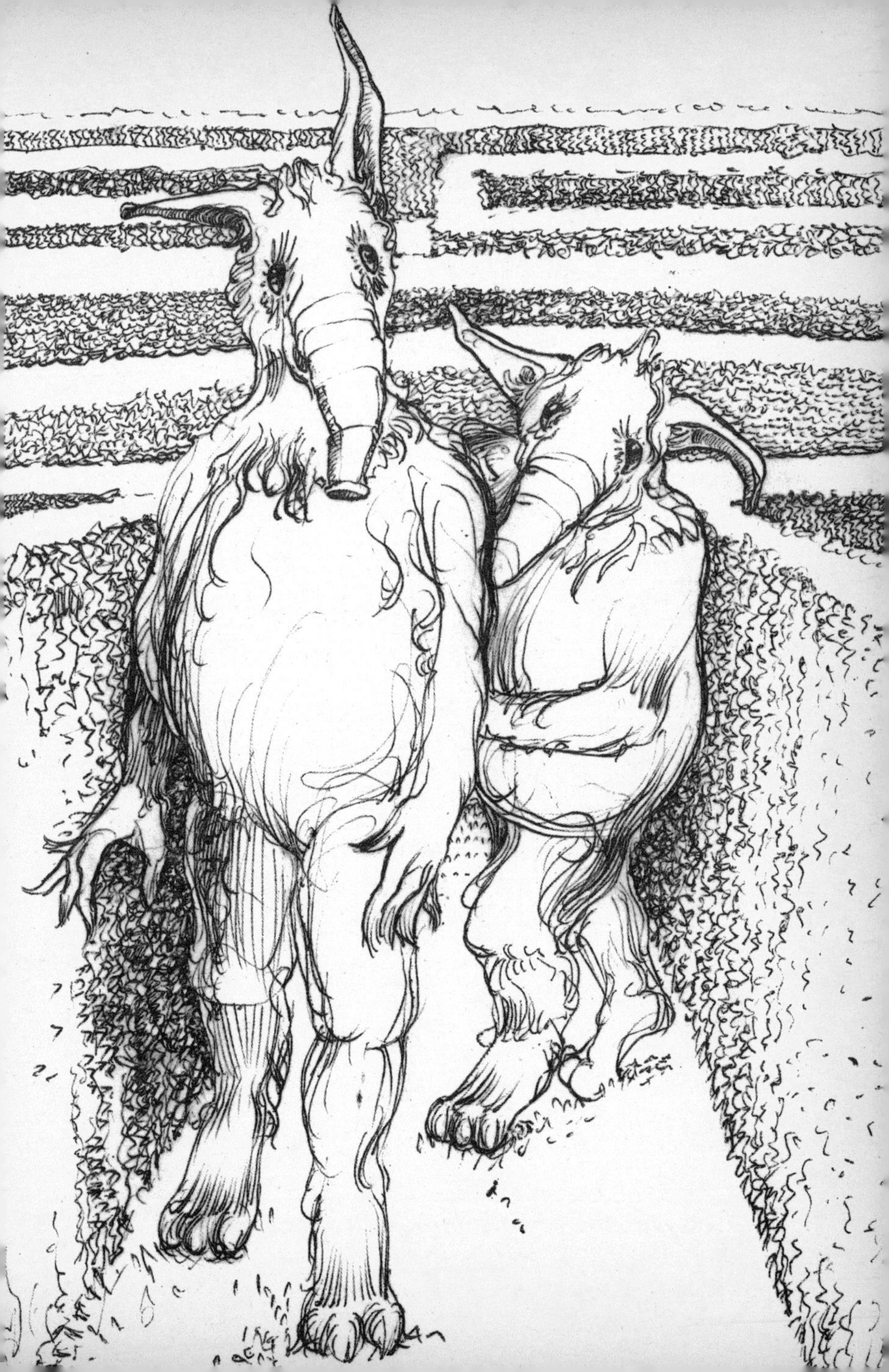

from page 116

Entering the hedge maze, you decide to use the brown thread. It is well camouflaged on the earthen path; the minotaur won't see it, but you will be able to retrace your steps with ease, knowing what to look for.

Wandering in the narrow green alleyways, you check each corner for a glimpse of Redfern. The path you are on ends in a T, so you peer right and left. The minotaur! He has rounded a bend and is coming your way!

You flatten yourself against a hedge, hoping that the monster doesn't turn into your alleyway. Luckily he does not see you as he stomps by, swinging his mace and munching on a fresh tristle. He vanishes around another corner.

Is the minotaur still tracking poor Redfern? you wonder. But *oh, no!* Here comes Redfern, nose to the ground, trailing the *monster!*

Waiting until your friend reaches the junction of the T, you grab him by the ear and drag him into your alleyway, then along your path of thread, and out of the maze.

"Redfern," you say, pushing him to the manor gate, "we've had quite *enough* tristles for one day!"

THE END

from page 40

Redfern doesn't look as if he's going anywhere. Maybe this is your chance to find your way out of the manor. You can always come back for your friend later.

You hurry after the mountain gnome, carefully keeping out of sight. Dropping a trail of red beans as you go, you follow the gnome through an underground maze and into a baffling series of gardens. Finally, as you had hoped, he leads you to the manor gate.

There he leaves his cart, and, wiping his hands and letting out a great puff of breath, he walks toward the manor house.

"Now for a nap!" he says to himself.

You wait patiently until he is gone, and you wait a little longer. Then, sneaking to the wooden cart, you drag it slowly along your trail of beans, hoping no one will notice the sound of its creaking wheels.

Redfern is sleeping on the storeroom floor, a foolish smile on his face. Heaving and huffing, you manage to load him onto the cart.

And, heaving and huffing, you haul your heavy load to the manor gate. Once in the fresh air, Redfern revives. He is suffering from a slight headache.

You flee through the gates, never having met the Master of Mazes.

THE END

from page 51

You decide to follow the marks of the tristle digger. The holes lead you deep into the wood.

But here you come upon a familiar rutted cart track, and soon meet the mystery tristler. Digging near a wooden cart is a mountain gnome, the same gnome you saw driving this same cart through the Master of Mazes' gate.

"Well, well," he says, straightening to look at you. "If it isn't a tristler from the far forest. What brings you here?"

"I am looking for my friend, Redfern," you answer. "He chased your cart through the gate to the manor. Have you seen him?"

"I might have," replies the gnome, a grin playing across his face. "But I must find my quota of tristles for the day. The Master will be angry if I don't bring back enough, you know. He *loves* tristles.

"Don't worry. The Master has probably taken a liking to your friend. He'll be safe for now. I'll make you a deal. If you work for me for the rest of the day, I'll help you both escape after sundown."

Is Redfern in the Master of Mazes' clutches? If so, it might be useful to have the help of an insider. But can you trust this gnome?

If you accept the gnome's offer, turn to page 108.

If you want to return to the manor house, turn to page 115.

from page 82

Dropping a trail of white pebbles on the earthen paths, you walk through the alleyways of greenery. At the dead ends you find, you leave little piles of pebbles.

At last you see Redfern a short way ahead of you.

Turn to page 118.

from page 60/from page 115

You, too, enter the hedge maze. But Sir Alf has disappeared. Did he go right or left?

Running to the end of the alleyway of greenery, you look in both directions. Too late to follow Sir Alf, you choose the turn to the left.

You wander in the maze, selecting turns at random. Often you come to a dead end and must reverse your steps.

Finally, rounding a corner into a long green alleyway, you find Redfern! But you also see Sir Alf over Redfern's shoulder, turning a corner at the end of the alleyway.

"Redfern! Come with me!" you shout. Redfern looks overjoyed to see you and begins to run in your direction.

"Redfern! My long-lost friend!" cries Sir Alf. Redfern turns in delight and scampers to meet Sir Alf.

"No, Redfern, come with *me!*" you yell.

"But it is *I*, Sir Alf," calls the knight.

Redfern halts in the center of the maze. Confused, he leans first one way, then the other. But the strain is too great. Torn by a choice he cannot make, whatever spell had created him is broken, and he vanishes into thin air.

Sadly, Sir Alf of Redfern takes his leave.

You will have to find your way out of the maze alone.

THE END

from page 78

You have used up your three clues, and you are still lost in a labyrinth somewhere in the manor house of the Master of Mazes. You have no choice but to try to guess his name.

"Maldor," you say. Nothing happens.

"Arnolf." Still nothing.

"Garth. Harold. Tristlemouth. Fernred," you say, guessing. "Marvin. Gamester. Abel. Baker. Claude. Donald. Edgar . . . ."

THE END

from page 52

Deciding to put the map to whatever use you can find for it, you tear it into small pieces and begin to wander in the maze again.

Whenever you enter a passage, you leave a scrap of paper on the floor to mark where you've been. And when you come to a dead end, you mark the passage with two scraps.

Sometimes you explore a turn, only to find yourself back in a passage already marked with a scrap. But finally your ingenuity pays off. You emerge from the green-marble maze, your map reduced to a few shreds.

You are in a large, paneled study, furnished with an overstuffed sofa and a graceful divan—a long, backless couch. The walls are lined with paintings and books.

Among several objects on a desk near the couch is a small crystal globe. The globe is filled with liquid. At the bottom is a snowy forest scene with a tiny figure standing among the trees.

You are about to shake the crystal, to watch the snowflakes swirl inside, when your hand freezes in mid-reach. For the figure in the snow crystal is *you!*

You cannot decide if you are curious or angry. What kind of trick is this?

If you want to shake the crystal, turn to page 106.

If you want to smash it open, turn to page 12.

from page 41

You abandon your search in the garden and head for the manor. Climbing up to a terrace at the back of the house, you find a pair of glass doors that open onto a ballroom.

"Redfern?" you call. There is no one about. But the chandeliers in the ballroom are ablaze with light.

The yellow shape reflected in the fountain was in a window at the top of the house. You decide to climb the sweeping marble staircase at one end of the ballroom.

The staircase spirals up for many stories. Finally you reach a landing in a dim hallway. The marble staircase ends, but you can see a flight of worn wooden steps leading to another door.

I *must* have climbed to the top of the house, you think, stopping to catch your breath. That door must lead to the attic.

The only furniture in the hallway is a huge grandfather clock. Its loud ticking fills the hall, and you note the time: five minutes short of the hour. There is a message fastened to its swinging pendulum:

So says the clock
Before a tock.

If you want to wait for the clock to strike, turn to page 45.

If you want to climb to the attic, turn to page 47.

from page 116

Entering the hedge maze, you decide to unroll the spool of white thread. The white will show up well on the earthen paths, you think, and it will be easier to follow.

You wander deep into the maze, noting that the white thread is, indeed, easy to see.

Unfortunately, the minotaur sees it, too. With a roar, he is upon you.

THE END

from page 90

Choosing the muddy path, you follow several deep impressions in the mud. They *are* paw prints.

But you soon find out to whom the paws belong. A bear!

The large brown bear is clawing at a tree a short distance from the path. In the tree, just beyond his reach, is a beehive.

The bear catches sight of you and growls. If he can't have a honeycomb, maybe a tasty tristler will do.

You still have a piece of fruit in your basket.

If you give the bear the fruit, turn to page 61.

If you throw the fruit at the hive to knock it loose, turn to page 100.

from page 82

Following the alleyways of greenery, you turn this way and that, guided only by your instincts.

And, at last, a short way ahead of you, you see Redfern!

Turn to page 118.

from page 110

Snick! Snee! Sir Alf's sword slashes through the dense thicket.

You must stay close behind him, because every opening Sir Alf can clear is soon overgrown again, and twice as thick.

Brambles scratch your face, and sticks catch your clothes. You feel as though you have been woven into a giant bird's nest.

Slash! With a final, flashing arc of his sword, Sir Alf breaks through the thicket maze, and you are free.

"Not so fast, *hee, hee!*" cries the Master of Mazes from a balcony of the manor house.

Suddenly you are surrounded by a second maze. This one is of rectangular halls of glossy white marble.

"My sword won't slice through marble," says Sir Alf doubtfully. "Should we use your pebbles in here?"

If you leave a trail of pebbles, turn to page 96.

If you can think of something else to use as a marker, turn to page 120.

from page 22

You decide to keep going. But you cannot find any lanes or paths in this labyrinth—just hexagonal rooms with arched doorways.

Thinking of the clue, you try taking the first exit in two-door rooms twice, then the last doors in the three-exit rooms thrice, but before long you are hopelessly confused, for some of the rooms have only one door and others have four, and you can hardly keep track.

Taking a deep breath, you try again. Suddenly you emerge in a room with six archways—a door in every wall. You must have reached the center of the maze!

You spot an envelope in the middle of the floor. "CLUE 3":

My name is hidden in the center
of this LABYRINTH.

You look around you. Surely there is nothing hidden in here. The room is bare.

If you can guess the Master of Mazes' name from this clue, turn to page 93.

If you need more clues, turn to page 69.

from page 29

Wasting no time, you make a beeline for the hedge maze.

"Redfern!" you call, dashing into the first green alleyway. Where could he have gone? You scurry this way and that, barely noticing the ceiling of hedges that is growing around you, cutting off your view of the sky.

All at once you catch sight of a wagging yellow tail. "Redfern!" you cry, hurrying toward the furry flag.

Redfern sadly looks up from the tristle hole he had tried to dig under one of the hedges. Prickly branches have grown all around him, and he is trapped.

Unfortunately, you too are soon engulfed as hedges twine about your arms and feet. Shoots of greenery grow to your knees, then to your shoulders. Twisting and bending, they outline your shape.

You and Redfern have just been added to the topiary zoo.

THE END

from page 31/from page 41

You follow the Redfern statue's pointing paw to the gazebo. It is a small round pavilion that looks like an ornament on a wedding cake. Slender columns support a domed roof. It is open to the air, and between the columns are rounded benches from which to admire the view.

Unfortunately, there is no sign of Redfern. Sitting on a bench, you wonder what to do next.

Suddenly you notice that your view is changing. The gazebo is spinning around! Faster and faster the scenery whips by—the manor, the fountain, an orchard, a garden, the manor, the fountain . . . .

You are thrown free of the spinning gazebo and stumble dizzily through a grove of trees. You have to sit for a moment to make your head stop spinning.

You must have landed in the orchard. Rows and rows of fruit trees stretch as far as you look.

Wandering through the maze of trees, you notice a tuft of yellow hair caught on a piece of bark. Redfern! A few feet away you find another tuft.

Turning in a circle, you look through the trees. You can no longer tell what direction you're going in in this orchard maze. You are hungry, and decide to pick some fruit.

But there is Redfern! He is scampering through the trees, many rows in the distance. You call to him, but he is out of earshot.

If you chase Redfern at once, turn to page 94.

If you first fill your tristle basket with fruit, turn to page 89.

from page 102

The minotaur has trapped you in his house, he has captured Redfern, and now he seems bound to kill you. You don't want to take any chances.

Gripping the sword in both hands, you face the charging minotaur.

With a loud cry—could it be a cry of delight?—the minotaur charges onto your sword.

But you feel no impact, and the minotaur vanishes into thin air. Could he have been a figment of your imagination?

Shrugging, you pull at your heavy helmet. It will not come loose!

Roaring with anger, you dash about the room, but the bull's head is stuck to your shoulders. The day passes and night falls.

You regard yourself in a mirror on one of the wardrobes. Then you dress yourself in a flowing cloak and set out to learn your way around this confusing manor.

For you are now the Master of Mazes.

THE END

from page 61/from page 90

Taking the path that is paved with white pebbles, you hope it will lead you to the garden. Along the way you fill your pockets with as many pebbles as you can carry.

The path leads to a wall of hedges, clipped into the shape of a familiar animal—Redfern! These topiary Redferns point to an opening in the hedge wall.

You soon discover that you have entered a maze of hedges. The hedge walls form alleyways of greenery that tower over your head. Here and there the bushy form of a topiary Redfern points to the right or the left.

The dirt paths twist and turn, and the figures of Redfern grow more fanciful. Here, he is lying on his back, pointing over one shoulder; there, he is standing on his head, pointing with one foot. But soon you come to a Redfern bush that points *both* ways.

Here we go again, you think, choosing the path to your right.

If you leave a trail of white pebbles, turn to page 67.

If you want to save the pebbles, turn to page 75.

from page 57

"Excuse me, Your Majesty," you say, bowing as best as an ant can. "My name is Lin the Tristler. I had no wish to intrude. But I am searching for my friend Redfern. Perhaps one of your subjects has seen him?"

"Find this 'Redfern' for our guest," the Queen commands. She chats to you pleasantly while ants scurry back and forth, busily rubbing antennae.

"Our chains of communication are surpassed by none," explains the Queen ant proudly. An exhausted messenger makes his report.

"Your friend is in the garden," says the Queen. "Our guards will show you out. Please give our regards to the Master of Mazes. For you are sure to meet him."

You emerge from the anthill with only a minute to spare. Then you feel a wave of dizziness, and you are back to your own shape again.

You had better get to the garden.

If you left a trail of acorns to follow, turn to page 117.

If you left a trail of pebbles, turn to page 19.

from page 34

You decide to follow the floor markings.

The pattern of arrows twists and turns, leading through rooms and halls. Finally you enter a game room. The arrows spiral to an end underneath a billiard table. Everywhere you look are games of skill. There is a chessboard set with strangely carved men, a wooden alley with a rack of ninepins, and tiddlywinks made of mother-of-pearl.

On the billiard table is a scroll which reads:

Welcome to my little game.
To win it, you must guess my name.
Find the labyrinth, find three clues.
After three, you'll surely lose.
Solve it in three—I'll set you free.
Solve it in two—your friend will join you.
Solve it in one—your quest is done.
signed, The Master of Mazes

The labyrinth is not hard to find, because a door at the end of the game room is clearly marked LABYRINTH. And beneath the door is an envelope labeled CLUE 1. You read:

Thou SHALT *not in* LABYRINTHS find my name!

If you can guess the Master of Mazes' name from this clue alone, turn to page 11.

If you need more clues, enter the labyrinth and turn to page 22.

IN
OUT

from page 112

You study the sign for a moment until its meaning becomes clear. The word Look is *under* the word Terrace. Look under terrace.

Following the clue, you skip down the flagstone steps and walk around to the side of the terrace. There, hidden in a hollow under the house, is Redfern!

Before you can utter a cry of joy, Redfern grabs your hand and pulls you under the terrace with him. He gestures for you to be quiet and wait.

Footsteps pound on the flagstones above your head. It is the minotaur. He is coming your way.

Drawing back into the shadows, you and Redfern watch as the minotaur stomps by. He is munching a fresh tristle and is carrying a large ring of keys. You hear him mumble to himself, "Those two won't escape *me.* I'll lock the front gate."

When the minotaur is out of earshot, you whisper to Redfern, "Can you track him down? We'll have to find a way to steal his keys."

Redfern nods. His nose is already at work, and you can tell he has zeroed in on the telltale tristle. He beckons you to follow.

Hiding behind a large bush, you watch as the minotaur locks the front gate. Then he stretches, and rubs his eyes.

"Let's hope he takes a nap," you whisper to Redfern.

The minotaur looks sharply in your direction, sniffing the air. But he does not see you and strides off to a small guardhouse near the front gate.

The sun is about to set. You wait patiently until you hear loud, bullish snores from the guardhouse.

Stealing quietly to the guardhouse door, you peer inside. Great snores shake the wooden building. The minotaur is asleep! With a series of gestures, you are able to make Redfern understand what you want him to do.

Stealthily, silently, Redfern snakes his long snout around the door and under the key ring at the minotaur's side. Slowly, gently, he lifts the ring, careful not to let the keys jingle.

Then, rapidly tiptoeing to the manor-house gate, you insert the key and make your escape, locking the gate from the outside in case the monster should wake.

"We did it!" you cry, as you and Redfern happily run home.

THE END

from page 46

The only place you can think of to find a cooked goose is in a kitchen. And from what you know of castles and manor houses, the kitchens and sculleries are usually on the lowest floor.

Exploring a simple hallway at the rear of the house, you soon locate a stone staircase leading down into shadows.

Your guess is correct. The staircase leads to several enormous kitchens, with enough great stoves and bread ovens to prepare three royal banquets daily. Like the rest of the house, all seems deserted.

Coming upon a generously stocked larder, you search for a goose but find only unopened bags of dried fruit and grains, stacked to the ceiling. One sack has burst its seams and overflows with red beans.

At the back of the larder you notice a door—probably to the wine cellars, you think. But then you are struck by an overpowering and familiar odor. Tristles!

Before you venture further, you fill your pocket with red beans. You are in a manor of mazes, after all, and you may need to leave a trail.

Turn to page 14.

from page 80

You stop to fill your tristle basket with fruit. You may be able to use them to mark a path if your search becomes a long one.

Then, following the tufts of yellow fur as best you can, you take off through the orchard in the direction of where you last saw Redfern.

Every way you turn it seems there is a fruit tree in your path. The rows have grown irregular, and you can no longer see very far.

Finally the orchard thins, and you come upon a large lake with a forest on the other side. You must be near the border of the estate.

A maze of covered bridges has been built across the lake. These curious wooden tunnels are so many, and so dense, that you can barely see water in some places.

Some of the longer bridges have windows in their walls, and tiny flags fly from their rooftops. The whole looks like a miniature city, crisscrossing the water.

Redfern must have headed for the forest, you think, walking onto the first wooden bridge.

Your footsteps clatter on the plank floor. The first bridge branches to the right and left. There is no trace of Redfern. You turn to the left, marking your choice with a piece of fruit from your basket.

The left tunnel curves for a way, then straightens out to shoot far ahead of you. Several windows light your path, but at each window another turn branches to the left or right.

From one window you can still see the shore. From another you see more covered bridges.

Taking turns at random, you mark each choice with a piece of fruit. When you reach dead ends, you leave two fruits, and retrace your steps to try another bridge.

Finally you emerge on the far side of the lake. The forest is vast. You look back at the maze of bridges. And there across the lake—oh, no. *Redfern!* You can just see his tiny figure as he skirts the orchard, heading back toward the garden!

Following your trail of fruit, you hurry back through the bridge maze. It is lucky you thought to bring that fruit. But you are too late. Redfern is gone.

You find the path that skirts the orchard. But this path soon splits in two. One path is muddy—but are those paw prints in the mud? The other path is paved with white pebbles.

If you take the muddy path, turn to page 74.

If you take the pebbled path, turn to page 82.

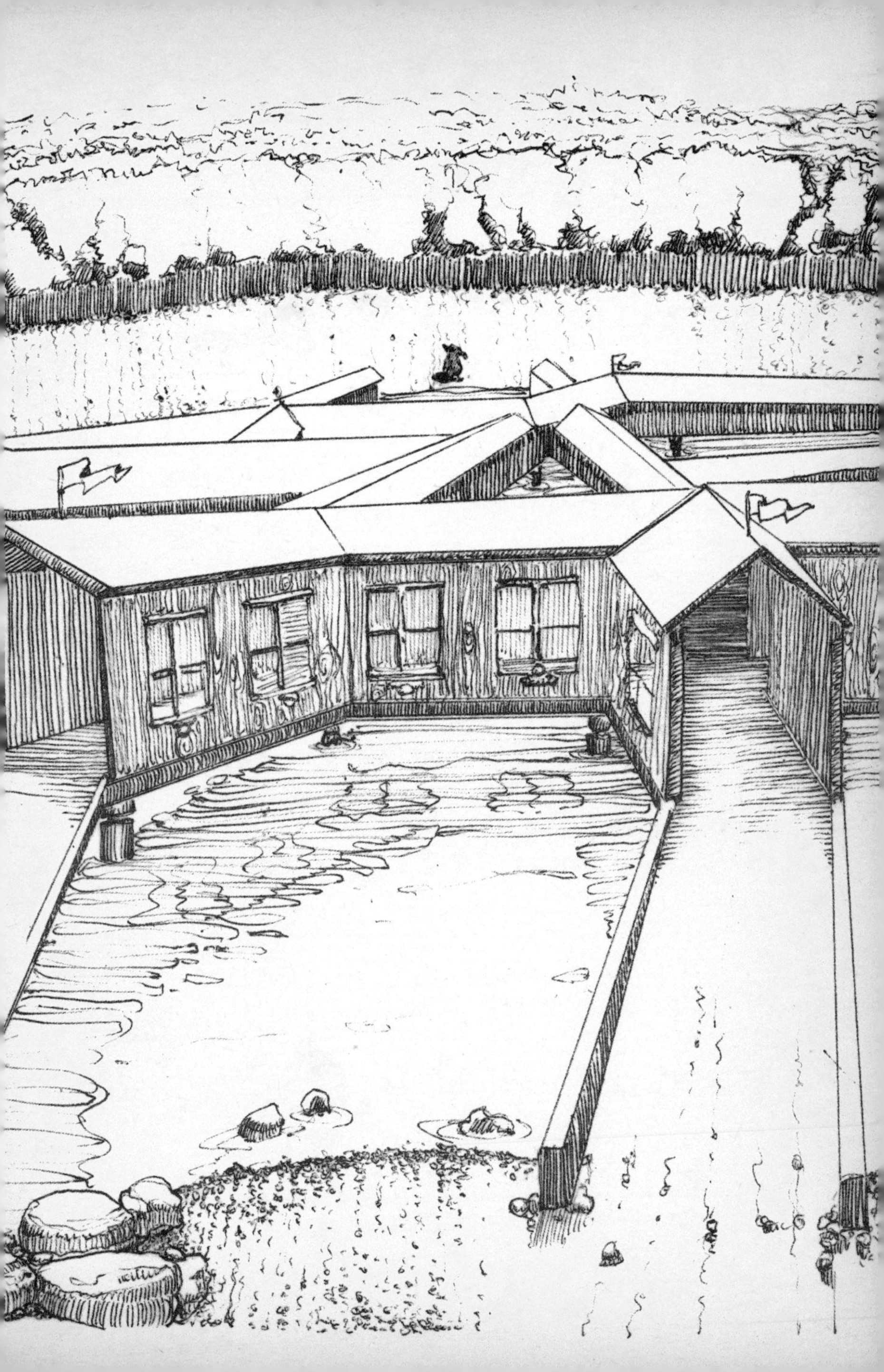

from page 18/from page 30

You puzzle through the picture message. A pot of tea, plus a cake, minus the letter "C": T + CAKE − C. Equals TAKE!

"Take the ——." Take the what? Stars with an eye in the center? No, stars with an "I" in the center! "STAIRS"! *Take the stairs!*

Excitedly you spring up the sweeping staircase at the end of the ballroom. You climb for many stories, until you reach a landing in a dim hallway. The marble staircase ends, and there is a flight of worn wooden steps leading to yet another door.

I *must* have climbed to the top of the house, you think, stopping to catch your breath. That must lead to the attic.

The only furniture in the hallway is a huge grandfather clock. Its loud ticking fills the hall, and you note the time: five minutes short of the hour. There is a message fastened to its swinging pendulum.

So says the clock
Before a tock.

If you want to wait for the clock to strike, turn to page 45.

If you want to climb to the attic, turn to page 47.

from page 78

This *must* be some kind of word game, you think. Perhaps the Master of Mazes' name is at the center of the *word* LABYRINTH.

"R," you guess. Nothing happens.

"YRI," you say. Again, nothing.

"BYRIN," you say aloud.

"Byrin is indeed my name," says a deep voice. "Solve it in three, I'll set you free."

In the blink of an eye, you find yourself back at the gate to the manor house.

You are free—but you still have to find Redfern.

THE END

Or, begin again on page 8.

from page 80

You take off after Redfern, zigzagging through the orchard maze. There always seems to be a fruit tree in your path, jumping in front of you, blocking your view.

"Blast these trees!" you say as you run, calling after Redfern.

But you have lost him, and you are quite lost yourself.

The orchard thins and you come upon a large lake with a forest on the other side. You must be near the border of the estate.

A maze of covered bridges crisscrosses the lake. These curious wooden tunnels are so numerous, and so dense, that you can barely see water in parts of the lake. Some of the longer bridges have windows in their walls, and tiny flags fly from their rooftops. It looks like a wooden city, stretched across the water.

And there, at the entrance to the maze, is a tuft of yellow fur. Trust Redfern to try to get to the forest, you think, as you walk onto the first wooden bridge.

Your footsteps clatter on the plank floor. The first bridge branches to the right and left. Redfern has left no trace. You turn to the right.

The next tunnel curves, and then straightens for a long way. Windows light your path at intervals, and at each window you find another branching bridge.

You stop to look out every window. From one you can still see the shore. But the bridge that branches away from it leads deeper into the maze. From another window you see only bridges, their rooftops looking darker as the day slowly fades.

Choosing turns at random, you are soon completely lost. You wish you had brought some fruit to eat. But perhaps Redfern will find *you*.

THE END

from page 76

Sir Alf follows as you wander through the white-marble halls, dropping a trail of pebbles to mark where you've been.

But the tiny white pebbles are impossible to see on the white-marble floors. And soon you are completely lost.

You hear the wicked laughter of the Master of Mazes:

"Maze Number Two—and I have caught *you!*"

THE END

from page 40

You are afraid to leave Redfern alone in this condition.

Fanning his face, you try to bring him to his senses.

"Redfern, snap out of it!" you say. But soon he collapses in a snoring heap, a foolish grin lighting his face.

The door to the storeroom slams open. It is the Master of Mazes! The mountain gnome cowers at his heels.

"What is this?" the Master of Mazes snaps angrily. "Tristles? *Tristles?* What do I want with all these tristles? I ordered *trestles*, not tristles. Trestles—for my new bridge maze." He stops short. "And who are *you?*"

"I am Lin the Tristler," you say meekly, and you tell your story.

"A tristler, eh?" says the Master of Mazes. "Then maybe *you* can use all of these tristles. *I* certainly can't. If you'll cart them away, you can keep them.

"And if you've gotten this far, you must be skilled at mazes, too. I could use a clever apprentice. Would you care to build some bridges?"

You think about his offer as you load the gnome's cart—with Redfern. Your friend revives, with only a slight headache, once you get him to the fresh air.

Then you fill the cart with a treasure in tristles and head toward home.

Your mind is made up. When you and Redfern return the empty cart to the manor, you'll stay awhile and see what you can learn from the Master of Mazes.

THE END

from page 12

Allowing your double to disappear into the secret passage, you turn your attention to the door hidden by Redfern's portrait. Behind it you hear a sorrowful weeping. And beyond the door you find Redfern!

Wailing with delight, he clasps you in a furry hug. You notice, with some amusement, that he smells of tristles, and he seems to have gained a bit of weight!

You are in an artist's studio, filled with easels and paints. The Master of Mazes has also been waiting for you in this room.

"Welcome, Lin the Tristler," he says. "And thank you for your help. Allow me to explain my secret. My paintings live. Your friend Redfern is an early creation of mine, made with colors mixed from essence of tristle. But now my speciality is mazes, for I have become a maze-ician of some renown. And I believe you have earned the rank of Master of Mazes yourself!"

His eyes twinkle merrily at the look of surprise on your face.

"You may leave or stay as you please, of course," he continues, turning to a fresh canvas.

You and Redfern eye each other. You are both wondering what the Master of Mazes will paint next.

THE END

from page 74

Aiming squarely at the beehive, you throw the fruit as hard as you can. Your aim is good, and the hive falls loose, bursting open in midair.

The bees swarm the hungry bear, stinging him through his thick fur. He thrashes his arms in the air and howls with anger and pain.

It seems you are safe from the bear for the moment. But now the bees spot you.

THE END

from page 50

This Master of Mazes thinks he's tricky, you think. But I can *really* confuse this game!

Standing before the mirror, you repeat the spell. Your reflection wavers and turns into Redfern's.

Hurrying out of the armory, you catch sight of the Master of Mazes—or Redfern—as he disappears into the hedge maze. You enter the maze, trying to remember the patterns you saw from the ballroom window. There should be a right, then another right and a left.

You reach the center of the maze. Two identical Redferns are staring at each other. And both turn in amazement to stare at *you*. You stare back. Which one is which?

Scampering between them, you wait expectantly. *Three* Redferns. Now what? There is a long silence.

"We shall have to have a tristling test," declares the Redfern on your right. "Only one of us can be the *real* Redfern." The Redfern on your left nods in agreement.

"Yes," you say, "only one of us is genuine, and it *isn't* me. The *real* Redfern can't talk!"

You grab hold of the Redfern on your left, but your precaution is not necessary. For the enchantment is broken. You are Lin again, and your host is himself.

"Well played!" says the Master of Mazes, laughing. "You win. And now you are both free to return home!"

THE END

from page 59

You decide to confront the monster. Arming yourself with a shining sword, you await the minotaur's attack.

The door to the armory slams open, and you are face to face with your enemy.

With a mighty roar, the minotaur hurls his mace at your head. You sidestep, sword drawn, and the mace crashes into a wall.

As you circle each other slowly, you size up your chances. You remember watching a troupe of acrobats who would grab a bull by the horns and vault over its back, landing safely behind. Are you that agile? The minotaur is larger than you, but his step is heavy and his movements are clumsy. And he is no longer armed.

Suddenly, lowering his head, the minotaur charges!

If you want to run him through with your sword, turn to page 81.

If you want to grab his horns and flip over his back, turn to page 104.

from page 57

You don't want to risk angering the Queen. Deciding to masquerade as the Master of Mazes, you approach the throne.

"Your Majesty," you say, trying to bow as best you can as an ant, "my mastery of mazes is but child's play compared to yours. The beauty of your tunnels is entrancing."

You seem to have said the right thing. For the Queen begins a lengthy speech about ant architecture, pausing only to ask, "Don't you agree?" You agree.

Suddenly you feel dizzy. Oh, no—your fifteen minutes are up!

You magically transform back to Lin the Tristler, and you are gigantic!

The mound of sand explodes around you and bits of ruby fly everywhere. Standing in the middle of the ruined anthill, you are swarmed by angry ants.

You hope that the *real* Master of Mazes shows up for his visit as planned—and soon!

THE END

from page 102

Dropping your sword, you charge at the charging minotaur, springing into the air as you grab his sharp horns. He raises his head in anger and surprise, and you are whipped through the air, up and over his back. Something gives—you hold on tightly! The minotaur's head pulls off in your hands!

You land on the floor behind him, rolling with the heavy head toward the door of the armory.

"My *power*, my *power!*" wails a thin voice. "I'll be lost in my own mazes!"

So *this* is the Master of Mazes, you think. A weak-faced man, no longer frightening, has collapsed in a heap on the floor. Clutching his bald head, he laments his loss. "My horns, my head!"

In your arms you hold the source of his power. You fit the minotaur's head onto your own shoulders.

Expecting a surge of power, you are surprised to feel no stronger. But the manor house no longer holds any mysteries. You walk directly to the hedge maze to rescue your friend Redfern.

THE END

from page 71

Curious, you lift the crystal and shake it gently. The snowflakes flurry wildly inside the globe, then drift thickly over the miniature forest. Snow settles on the tiny trees and clings to the hair of the miniature Lin.

But what is that icy feeling at the back of your neck? It is snowing in the study!

At first there are just a few flakes. But soon you are standing in a swirling snowstorm, and the study is fading from sight. The paneled walls have turned to trees, and the overstuffed sofa is now a bank of snow.

The crystal globe has turned to solid ice, and you drop it into the carpet of snow that once was the floor of the study. The chunk of ice skitters past your feet and down a steep hill and disappears in the distant whiteness. Why is the hill so icy, you wonder, when it is snowing so hard?

You look again—and can just make out a slick toboggan track zigzagging along the hill. The ridges of the track make a maze of icy paths, hard to see clearly in the now raging blizzard.

You see a lump in the snow nearby. The divan! It has become a curl-fronted sled—a toboggan!

Should you try to negotiate the hazardous toboggan track? Surely the blizzard will end soon. Your teeth chatter with the cold.

If you want to ride the toboggan, turn to page 27.

If you want to wait for the storm to blow over, turn to page 55.

from page 54

You join the teeming line of ants in the downward tunnel. After an exhausting march, you emerge in a cavernous space. It is so enormous that you can hardly tell where you are.

You have left your sandy tunnel and are walking on rock. The ants stream by a flaming tree—no, it must be a torch—and begin to pick up slivers of red glass. Ruby chips!

Suddenly you feel yourself falling! For a moment all goes dark. Then you are your normal size again. Your fifteen minutes must be up.

You are in a ruby mine, far underground. On a nearby wall, next to a blazing torch, a line of tiny ants struggle to carry ruby chips back into their tunnel.

It looks as if the mine has not been used for years. You fill your pockets with rubies—they may be useful if you find yourself in another maze. And you wouldn't mind returning home with a treasure!

The mine proves to be a maze of fallen beams and abandoned train tracks. But you follow one of the rusty tracks to a storeroom. There you notice a familiar smell. Tristles!

You must be back in the manor house. Feeling your pockets, you sigh with disappointment. For the rubies have somehow turned to red beans.

Turn to page 14.

from page 66

"I agree," you tell the gnome.

"Then get to work," he says, snapping his fingers. "There's no time to lose. Dig over there."

"B-but . . ." you begin.

"No buts. Just dig." He hands you his spade and leans against a tree to watch.

Shrugging, you follow the gnome's orders. But he has asked you to dig under a butternut tree. You *know* there won't be any tristles there.

"Deeper, deeper," urges the gnome. "I have a feeling about this spot."

A deal is a deal. You dig and dig, until you are almost ready to drop from exhaustion. Still the gnome presses on, until you are standing in a hole so deep, you can no longer see him unless he leans over the edge.

Propping your arms on the handle of your spade, you stop to rest. Clods of earth and twigs have fallen into your hair and clothing. You wipe your forehead, leaving a streak of dirt from your muddy hand.

"How much further?" you call to the gnome. "I'm telling you, tristles grow only under *oaks!*"

Your only answer is the clatter of cartwheels. You are stuck in a deep hole in the forest, tricked by the evil gnome.

THE END

from page 62

The first Redfern is hugging you like a long-lost friend. And the second Redfern is clutching the first as though he doesn't want him to get away.

You decide that the first Redfern must be the real one.

"Redfern!" you cry, hugging him back.

"Not so!" says the Master of Mazes, transforming back to his human shape. "I simply grabbed you to fool you. But your friend here is after the tristles in my pockets!"

You can see that he speaks the truth. Redfern has his snout well into the Master's coat pocket and is paying scant attention to anything else.

"Well," says the Master of Mazes, politely ignoring Redfern, "I hope you have enjoyed my little game. But I have won, and now I shall claim my prize."

Your heart leaps. Does he want Redfern?

"I shall gladly show you and your friend back to my gates—and you shall reward me with a year's supply of tristles. Deal?"

"Deal!" you reply.

THE END

from page 20

You decide to team up with Sir Alf. After all, two may be able to find Redfern twice as fast as one.

"I have already searched the forest," says Sir Alf. "Let's pay a visit to this Master of Mazes." You set off for the manor house.

Walking quietly through the garden, you approach the back of the manor.

"*Hee, hee, hee,*" cackles a voice from an upper window. "Do you think you can sneak up on *me*?"

It is the Master of Mazes! His face is twisted in an evil leer. And behind him, in a golden cage, is Redfern! The Master of Mazes calls to you again.

"Here's a challenge for you, my fine knight! And for you too, tristle poacher! *If you find your way through my mazes three, you can take your silly friend —and I'll set you free!*"

He casts a maze of thickets around you and the knight. You are trapped in a dark nest of brambles and briars. And the brambles seem to be everywhere—around you, above you, even under your feet.

"I still have my pockets filled with pebbles," you say. "We can start walking out of the maze and leave a trail to mark where we've been."

"By Jove, I'll slash our way out with my sword!" cries Sir Alf.

If you think Sir Alf should use his sword, turn to page 76.

If you want to use your pebbles, turn to page 53.

from page 52

You decide you had better save the map in case you need it later. Surely if you wander long enough, you will find your way out of this maze.

Everywhere you look is the same green marble—ceiling, walls, and floor. You feel as though you are at the bottom of the ocean.

You walk and walk, twisting left or right. Sometimes you come to a dead end of solid wall and must go back the other way. Other times you notice patterns in the marble that you think you have seen before.

When you are tired, you stop to sleep. When you are hungry, meals magically project from the walls. At least the Master of Mazes is proving to be a generous host. The food is always excellent. Often there are tristles.

You have lost track of time, but you think you have eaten ten or eleven meals when you encounter a sleeping yellow form. Redfern!

After a joyous reunion, you wander through the maze together. Finally, one day, there is a new kind of light at the end of a passage. The forest! You are free!

You are not certain how long you have been gone. But you walk slowly now, and stooped, while Redfern's fur is long and gray.

THE END

from page 42

You race through the manor house in search of an exit to the garden. What a confusing house! Doorways open to solid walls, and windows turn out to be mirrors. Fireplaces are filled with ferns, and furniture hangs from the ceiling. There are ladders that lead nowhere and carpets patterned like sky and clouds.

Entering a small sewing room, you pause to catch your breath. It crosses your mind to grab two spools of thread. You may need to leave a trail to find your way out of the hedge maze—if you can find a way there, that is.

Running down a flight of stairs, you come to a dead end. You run back up, and up another flight, but the up stairs take you downward. You are in a maze of stairs!

Spotting a flight of flagstone steps, you try to climb up—and land outdoors on the flagstone terraces you had seen from the ballroom window. The hedge maze is ahead of you. A sign to your left says:

TERRACE
LOOK

If you want to search the terrace, turn to page 86.

If you head straight for the maze, turn to page 116.

from page 62

You pause to think. There is only one thing in the world that Redfern loves more than you—tristles. And the Master of Mazes was eating one as he entered the armory.

Taking a chance, you disengage yourself from the first Redfern's hug and embrace the second.

"Redfern!" you cry. The real Redfern hugs you back.

"Well played, Lin the Tristler," says the Master of Mazes. "You win!"

The owner of the manor has regained his true form. He pulls several tristles from his pocket. "These were my downfall," he says ruefully.

"Ours, too!" you admit, laughing.

Redfern nods happily. He has had a successful tristling day.

THE END

from page 66

You don't trust this sly-looking gnome. And if what he says is true, Redfern may be in danger.

You decide you'd better hurry back to the manor house and look for the Master of Mazes.

As you enter the garden, you spot Sir Alf disappearing into a high maze of hedges.

The manor house looms to your right.

If you want to enter the manor, turn to page 32.

If you want to follow Sir Alf into the maze, turn to page 68.

from page 112

You head directly for the maze, hoping the minotaur has not yet found Redfern. A well-trampled dirt path leads into the alleyways of hedges. There are no footprints.

You are about to enter the maze when you remember the thread you took to mark your path.

Digging into your pockets, you pull out two spools of thread, one brown and one white.

If you unroll the brown thread, turn to page 64.

If you use the white thread, turn to page 73.

from page 39/from page 83

Once again you set off through the maze of tree roots, following acorns this way and that. But they seem awfully close together. Could you have dropped as many markers as that?

You look for signs of tristle holes, but leaves have fallen everywhere.

The wind starts up again. Leaves rustle and swirl, and branches creak overhead. More acorns spatter the forest floor like splashing raindrops.

You are completely lost.

You can only hope that it is not too late to begin using the white pebbles.

THE END

from page 67/from page 75

Redfern is standing at the center of the hedge maze. Overjoyed to see you, he runs to your side.

You are so relieved to find him well that you almost overlook his companion. For beyond Redfern stands the Master of Mazes!

"Well done, Lin the Tristler," says the princely man. "You have found us at last! I am Byrin, the Master of Mazes. And I am the maker and master of Redfern as well."

Your heart sinks. Does he want Redfern back?

"I hope you have enjoyed your travels on my little estate," says Byrin. "I have long hoped to meet as able a student as you, and I thank you for bringing Redfern back to me.

"But it would not be fair to ask him to choose between us. And I would like to reward you. I propose that you and Redfern hunt tristles for half the year. For the other six months, you can both live with me, and I shall teach *you* to be a Master of Mazes. When I retire, my estate shall be yours. What do you say?"

It takes only one look at Redfern's eager face. You agree to the Master's plan.

"And," says Byrin, "if you were wise enough to leave a trail of white pebbles to get here, we can start right away. Otherwise, for your first exercise, you will have to find your way out of this maze!"

THE END

from page 76

"I think we should save the pebbles," you tell Sir Alf. "Besides, they'll be too hard to see on this white floor. We'll have to think of something else to use as a marker."

"My armor?" suggests Sir Alf, though not too eagerly.

"There aren't enough pieces," you assure him. "And you may need it later. I know! Lend me your sword!"

Carefully slicing the bottom off your bright red shirt, you soon have a handful of little cloth squares, and a few red buttons as well.

You and Sir Alf explore the maze of marble halls, leaving a marker at every turn. When you come to a red marker, you can tell you have been that way before, and you choose another direction.

At last you emerge from the final marble hall. You are almost to the Master of Mazes' front gate!

"*Hee, hee,* not so fast," the Master of Mazes cackles.

A *third* maze springs up around you. You find yourselves in midair, far above the manor roof. The maze is made of glass tubes, too thick to shatter but so clear you can barely see where one wall ends and another begins. At the very bottom of the maze, waiting near the gate, is Redfern.

You feel your way along the glass tubes. But openings look the same as walls, and holes lead to dead ends.

A pebble drops from your pocket and clatters through the tube of glass. It rolls to an opening and disappears.

"Sir Alf!" you say excitedly. "It's time to use the pebbles!"

One by one you release the little stone markers. Through the maze they rattle and bounce, guiding you downward to Redfern.

The last pebble rolls out of the last glass tube, and the gate to the manor swings open. You win! You are free!

Redfern hugs you joyfully. Then he hugs Sir Alf. Your heart skips a beat. Have you come all this way to lose your friend to the knight?

"Sir Redfern of Redfern," says Sir Alf, bowing low to your friend. "When you left our kingdom to seek adventure in the world, you forgot your golden collar. I hereby return it to you."

Redfern bows in return and fastens the collar about his throat. It allows him to speak!

"Onward we go, Lin the Tristler," he cries in a gruff voice, "for more adventures await us, I am sure!"

THE END

from page 29

You stop to fill your pockets with pebbles so you can leave a trail through the hedge maze. Entering the narrow alleyways of greenery, you turn this way and that, calling Redfern's name. Every few yards you drop a tiny white pebble to mark where you've been.

Finally you round a turn and find yourself at the center of the maze, face to face with the Master of Mazes. And at his side is Redfern. Your friend clasps you in a welcoming hug.

"Well done, Lin the Tristler," says the Master of Mazes. "I have long been searching for a student as clever as you. I now award you the honorary degree of Master Maze-ician, Level One." He pins a gold medallion to your coat.

"You are free to leave for home right away, of course," he continues. "But if you and Redfern will return each spring as my apprentices, you shall inherit my manor and all of my lands."

You need some time to consider such an offer. But Redfern nods excitedly. After all, these are the best tristling grounds in the whole Forgotten Forest.

THE END